FESTIVAL FAIRY TALES

COLLECTION TWO

Printed in Russia for the publisher
Peter Haddock Limited, England

CONTENTS

THIS BOOK BELONGS TO

Once upon a time, there was a very naughty little girl. Her greatest wish was to become a witch. But not a good little witch. No. A bad little witch!

She began to read more and more books to find out how to become a witch.

"When I have become a witch, I shall be able to make all kinds of spells, and what fun I shall have," thought the little girl.

When she had read lots of books, she found one which said quite clearly, that in order to become a "know-all" of a witch, it was necessary to wear a witch's costume.

"I can soon arrange that," said the little one to herself.

She went up to the attic and from an old trunk she took some ancient clothes, which she turned into a lovely witch's costume.

She also hired a little owl to assist her with her mischievous plans.

"That's it, and now to work!"

A sly cat was watching her intently, but he hid under the table — to keep out of the way of the flies.

"Ha, ha, ha! What fun I shall have, playing tricks on the other children!"

The "novice" witch began to prepare a potion, and so that it would come out properly enchanted, she poured into the cauldron all kinds of unpleasant mixtures.

The little animals of the wood were very frightened when they saw such diabolical looking smoke coming out of the chimney.

"There's something evil cooking in that house!" they said to one another.

But there she was, casually stirring and stirring away at that mysterious potion, and what did she see?

"Oh! what's this? What's happening?"

What was happening, dear children, was that all the pots and pans that were touched by the smoke given off by the cauldron were coming to life.

"Oh, what have I done? That was not what I intended!"

But the cups, coffee pots, spoons and brooms, were all beginning to dance and jump around the little girl.

As if they were dancing to the sound of some mysterious music, they could not stop whirling round and looking menacingly at the little witch.

It was such an horrendous sight, that even the owl and the mice wanted to hide.

As the little girl did nothing to put right what was wrong, the crockery started to bump into her.

"Ow!" cried the little girl, for it hurt. But turning deaf ears, the pots merely poked her all the more.

The bad thing was that the poor owl too got his share and exclaimed very angrily, "So you wanted to amuse yourself casting spells on others did you? Now just look what you've done!"

The little girl pronounced the magic words that would put an end to magic spells for ever more!

She quickly got out of the witch's outfit and, very sorry for having had such wicked thoughts, she went out into the garden to play in the sun and the fresh air.

That served as a lesson to her and made her understand that one should not do to others what one would not like to have done to oneself.

CINDERELLA

Cinderella was a lovely maiden, whose stepmother and stepsisters were jealous of her beauty. They made her work all day long, washing and scrubbing, because they thought that was the way to make her uglier.

But she was helped in her burdensome toil by her friends, the little animals of the wood.

One day they received an invitation from the King to attend the Palace ball. Her stepmother said to Cinderella, "You can stay at home and do the washing up and the cleaning."

The wicked stepmother did not want the lovely Cinderella to go to the festivities in case the Prince noticed her.

Poor Cinderella was very sad when she saw her stepmother and stepsisters leave in all their finery to enjoy themselves at the ball.

A tear fell from her beautiful eye. Immediately her Fairy Godmother appeared and said to her, "Don't cry Cinderella. You shall go to the Palace ball."

"How can I when I haven't a dress?" asked the young maiden.

"Never fear!" replied the fairy. "You shall wear the prettiest dress and you shall be the most beautiful of all!"

The fairy touched her with her magic wand, whereupon the rags Cinderella was wearing turned into a beautiful gown.

"You must come back before midnight," warned the fairy, "because at that hour the spell will disappear."

When she arrived at the Palace and got down from her majestic coach pulled by six white horses, everyone at the festivities was dumbfounded.

"Who can this beautiful lady be?" wondered her stepsisters, who had not recognized her.

The Prince, when he saw her, was so captivated by her beauty that he danced the whole evening with her.

"I must go back before midnight," thought Cinderella, "otherwise the coach will turn back into a pumpkin and the six white horses into six mice, as they were before the fairy touched them with her magic wand." But Cinderella felt so happy dancing with the Prince that she forgot everything else.

When she heard the clock strike twelve, she ran from the Palace, dropping a slipper as she went.

The Prince, taken aback by the flight of the young lady, ran after her and picked up the slipper.

Some days later a page set out to travel throughout the kingdom, with orders to find the owner of the other glass slipper.

Cinderella's stepsisters also tried to put on the little slipper . . . . but it was made to fit only Cinderella.

The stepsisters were amazed when they saw Cinderella take out the other slipper to match.

And so it happened that the Prince married Cinderella and the two of them lived happily ever after.

That was the reward Cinderella received for all the sacrifices she made and the hardships she endured with goodness and self-denial.

JACK AND THE BEANSTALK

Once upon a time, there was a boy they called Jack of the Beanstalk. They called him that because one day he went to market and exchanged his cow for a handful of fine beans.

When he arrived home he planted them in his garden in the hope that they would bring forth good fruit.

However, the next day when he woke up, great was his amazement when he saw that the beans had grown so quickly that they reached up to the sky.

Jack climbed up the stalk of his plant. He went up and up until he was higher than the clouds. His house looked very tiny down there in the distance.

When he reached the top of
his gigantic plant, he spied a
castle in which there lived an
enormous giant.

Jack, who was very brave, entered the castle and saw the giant, who was sitting listening to music and watching a hen laying golden eggs.

Jack marvelled and thought that if he had such a hen, there would be no more poverty in his house.

"Please Sir, will you lend me the hen that lays the golden eggs?" said he to the ogre.

By way of reply, the giant seized him and was about to put him in his lunchtime sandwich.

But Jack, who was very agile, jumped like a flea, seized the hen and began to run back to the beanstalk.

The giant set off after him, but the beanstalk swayed back and forth under his great weight.

Jack reached the ground first and, taking an axe, cut down the beanstalk at a single stroke.

The giant came down with such a bump that he no longer had the will to pursue him.

With the golden eggs laid by the hen, Jack was able to bring happiness to all the poor people in the town.

TOM THUMB

One day, Tom Thumb, who was the smallest of seven brothers, heard his parents sadly saying to one another, "We shall have to abandon the children in the forest, because we have no money and no work."

The next day, they sent them to seek firewood in the thickest part of the forest, in the hope that they would get lost.

Tom Thumb, who knew that, dropped crumbs of bread to guide them home again.

However, during the night the crumbs disappeared. The birds had eaten them.

The children began to cry, but Tom Thumb climbed up a tree and spied a castle in the distance.

When they arrived at the castle, they knocked several times at the door, but nobody came.

The children were very tired and lay down to sleep. Tom Thumb, however, was awoken by the sound of footsteps.

Tom Thumb saw an enormous giant, who said to himself as he counted them, "How tasty these seven children will be fried in a sauce!"

Hearing this, Tom Thumb awoke his brothers and said to them, "We must get away from here. Run! It is the giant coming to eat us up!"

The boys fled in terror.

They ran and ran, so far, that the giant became very tired. He lay down to rest and soon fell asleep.

Tom Thumb took advantage of this to take off the seven league boots which the giant was wearing. Without them he was only an ordinary little man.

Tom Thumb took the seven league boots to the King, and he rewarded him with a purse full of gold for having freed the country from such a fearsome ogre.

With the gold, they went home to their parents who had repented and welcomed them with open arms.

Thanks to Tom Thumb, they all lived happily ever after.

WILD BLOSSOM

Wild Blossom was a little orphan girl who had to look after and feed her little brothers.

The only way she could make a living was to go into the country and pick pretty posies of flowers, which she then sold. She and her little brothers lived on the money she earned.

But one day, when she had picked more flowers and was ready to go to market and sell them, she felt poorly.

"Oh dear me! How poorly I feel."

Little Wild Blossom felt very cold and had to wrap herself in an old shawl.

"I have got the shivers, I must have a fever. I cannot go and sell my flowers today," said she to her little brothers. "I have such a headache."

How sad the little ones were to see their sister poorly in bed.

"My poor little flowers," said Wild Blossom between naps. "If I don't sell them today, tomorrow they will be withered away."

But lo! While our little girl was sleeping, the gardeners from the sky stealthily appeared. Equipped with heavenly dew and petal transplant, they worked on those flowers that the little girl had so lovingly picked. They achieved a miracle and the flowers did not fade, so that she would be able to sell them when she was better.

When she had been ill for a few days, Wild Blossom woke up one morning and felt that the fever had gone. Her head had stopped aching and she felt better.

Her joy was doubled when she saw that the flowers she had picked some days before were still fresh and flourishing.

"It's a miracle! I shall be able to sell them and earn some money!"

The little girl looked with eyes full of wonder at the baskets full of flowers.

"They really are marvellous flowers," she said to herself. "They are heavenly!"

For what had happened was that the heavenly gardeners had given each flower a radiance and each leaf an everlasting glow.

That day, Wild Blossom's flower stall was resplendent as never before.

"Give me a posy of those golden daisies," said one customer.

"Make me a bunch of these marvellous roses," said another.

Soon she had sold them all and could have sold more besides. The little girl was very happy and contented.

And so it was that Wild Blossom got home with her basket full of food for her dear little brothers who were waiting joyfully for her.

"Look brothers what I've got! I sold all the flowers and have bought lots of things!"

And that was how the heavenly gardeners rewarded this little girl for being so good and working so hard.

THE DONKEY SKIN

Rosalind was a very cheerful and nice little girl, always ready to help others. Which is why all the woodland animals loved her so much.

The little girl lived in an old castle with her stepmother and her horrible daughter.

Rosalind's stepmother was jealous of her beauty, which is why she made her do all the heaviest work, in the hope that she would grow as ugly as her own ugly daughter.

One day, the stepmother and her daughter went to town to buy warm clothes because winter was coming.

Her stepmother, instead of buying an overcoat for Rosalind, bought her a donkey skin, knowing full well that once she had put it on, she would be unable to take it off again.

"Here, this is all you are worth," she said to her.

The little girl had no alternative but to put it on, and that was how her stepmother succeeded in making her uglier than her own daughter.

Her step sister was very happy and contented when she saw how everyone laughed at Rosalind and called her Donkey Skin.

"Look who's here! Donkey Skin! Donkey Skin!" they cried.

Some time later, when she found that she could not take off the donkey skin, and was tired of being the butt of everyone's laughter, she decided to flee through the forest.

Rosalind was crying, when a Prince with a magic lute happened to pass that way.

At the sound of his melody, little by little, the donkey skin started to fall away, until she was free of it.

Whereupon, the Prince was so astonished by the beauty of Rosalind, that he decided to carry her off to his Palace and marry her, and they lived happily ever after.

ANDY AND HIS ACCORDION

Once upon a time, there was a very merry boy called Andy.
He travelled about from town to town playing his accordion.
In that way he was able to earn good money to feed himself
and his faithful dog.

One day, he arrived at a small town that had a very fine square.

Andy took his faithful old accordion from his bundle and got ready to begin his wonderful concert.

Andy thought that in such a pretty place as that, there must live some nice people who would enjoy good music and he hoped to earn enough money to last him for some time.

However, it did not turn out quite like that.

When he started to play — what a horrible noise came out of his accordion!

"Oh! What has happened?" exclaimed Andy.

A shower of rotton food and old rubbish was Andy's reward for his concert.

His old accordion had gone out of tune. It had been played and played so much that air was escaping from the bellows and making such horrible whistling noises.

Enormous tears fell from his eyes and ran down his cheeks.

"What will become of me and my dog," wondered Andy sadly.

So that night they had to sleep out in the open because they had no money to pay for lodgings.

But lo! A little angel from heaven took pity on them and poured into the accordion the sounds of celestial music.

Whereupon, the old accordion recovered its strength and started to play again, fantastically, or rather it played like the angels themselves!

That morning, when Andy started to play his accordion, the whole town came running to hear him.

"What an angelic sound," exclaimed a little girl, spellbound by the sound of the music coming out of that accordion.

From then on, our little friend was listened to most attentively in all the towns he visited.

Such was his success, that with the money he earned, he was able to buy himself a caravan, and never had to travel on foot again, thanks to that little angel who took pity on him in his misfortune.

Joanna was a very good girl, but she was very poor. Such was her poverty, that sometimes she only had a crust of bread, and would hand that over if anyone asked for it.

As she was so good, one day a magician gave her a beautiful white hen.

The next day, Joanna went to see if the hen had laid an egg for her breakfast and . . . what a surprise! The hen had laid an egg — but it was made of solid gold.

She was very pleased with it and took it straight to show her mother, and together they went to the jeweller's to sell it.

With the money they received for that precious egg, they were able to buy many things they lacked — food, clothes, shoes and other articles.

From that day forward,
Joanna was a rich and
disagreeable little girl, who on
one occasion, even threw out
of her house a little boy who
asked for a crust of bread.

64

But the day after she had treated the boy so badly, when Joanna went to collect the golden egg laid by the hen — what a disappointment! All she found were lovely fat fried eggs.

''What's this! Where are the golden eggs?'' asked Joanna angrily.

"Cluck, cluck, cluck," said the hen.

"I'll give you cluck, cluck, cluck, you bad hen! Aren't you ashamed at laying such rubbish?" shouted Joanna.

And she began to beat the hen with her broom. The poor bird was very frightened by the rage of her mistress.

But the next day, the magician appeared to her again and said, "It is not the fault of your hen that it is not laying golden eggs. It is your bad behaviour in not being charitable to the poor, and I have punished you. It will not lay any more golden eggs until you change your ways."

Joanna was very sorry and ashamed and she understood that it was a punishment she well deserved. She ran out in search of the poor boy she had turned away a few days before and invited him in to eat.

From then on, the hen continued to lay the golden eggs, which she distributed to all the poor children of the town.

NON-STOP TO THE MOON

There was once a very nice old man who drove a picturesque little train that ran round an amusement park.

Every day he went round and round the park, but he dreamed of going to the moon in his little train.

"The train's run right away!" exclaimed a very surprised little girl.

And so it was that . . .

. . . one day, to the amazement of everyone, the train went up in the air and started to fly – non-stop to the moon!

The little old man gazed at the houses getting smaller and smaller in the distance.

He could not contain his joy at being able to see all these wonderful things from the sky.

He flew and flew. He left our world far below him and the stars greeted him as he passed by.

"I'm going to the moon!" cried the old man excitedly.

Suddenly he found himself in front of his friend the moon and asked her, "Lady Moon, would you please allow me to run my little train round your stately surface?"

The moon was delighted to have a visitor and, smiling broadly, agreed.

The old man was so grateful that he invited some moon people, who were gazing at his earthly vehicle in amazement, to come for a ride in his jolly little train.

"Who can this funny creature be?" wondered the inhabitants of the moon.

But their curiosity got the better of them and they climbed aboard this very strange "gadget" puffing out smoke and saying, "Chuff! Chuff! Chuff!"

The moon gazed happily at the little old man driving his engine and carriages contentedly.

He went round and round her and the moon people enjoyed themselves just as much as children do on earth.

"What fun!" they cried.

And they would have gone on for much longer if . . . the good man's dream had not been interrupted by the sound of the bell, rung by one of his passengers which woke him from his slumbers.

What a pity that it was all a dream!

There was once an old miller, who died and left the little he had to his three sons. To the youngest of the brothers all he left was his cat.

"What on earth can I do with a cat?" said he to himself.

The cat heard what he said and replied, "Master, give me a pair of boots and you will see how clever I am!"

As soon as his master gave him the boots, the cat ran through the streets shouting, "My master is going to marry the King's daughter!"

The first thing he did
was to go hunting
for a plump rabbit.
He used a juicy
carrot for bait, and —
Zap! — one fell
straight into the trap.

When he had caught the rabbit, he bowed before the King and said to him, "Great King, my lord the Marquis has sent me with this gift for you."

"And what is your master's name?" asked the King.

"The Marquis of Carabas!" replied the cat solemnly.

The next day, the cat, proceeding with his plan, said to his master, "Have a bathe in this river while I go in search of the King."

The young man did not know what was going on, but he obeyed and dived into the water.

Puss in Boots knew that the King would be passing by that place and went out to meet him.

When he caught sight of his carriage he began to shout, "The Marquis of Carabas has been robbed! They stole my master's clothes while he was bathing!"

The King stopped the procession and went down to the river. When he saw the unfortunate plight of the Marquis he began to give orders.

"Bring forth fine clothes for my good friend the Marquis of Carabas."

The cat's master then realized how fortunate he had been to inherit such a cunning animal.

When the King saw what a good-looking young man he was he believed him to be a great nobleman and decided he should marry his daughter.

And so it was that Puss in Boots made his master a rich man who lived happily ever after with his Princess.

There was once a most ambitious and miserly King. His aim in life was to amass more and more gold and he paid no attention whatever to the needs of his people.

Not satisfied with the gold he already had, one day, he called upon a famous magician.

"I want you to use your magic to make my treasures multiply!" he said.

"I will give you extraordinary power, such as no mortal ever had nor ever will have," said the magician to him. "Hold out your hand!"

The magician gently tapped the hands of his sovereign and said, "From this moment onwards everything you touch will turn into gold."

And that was how everything the King touched was transformed into purest gold.

But when he went to eat, he saw to his surprise that all the food he touched also changed into gold.

He was not at all pleased about that, for if it continued he would starve to death.

The next day, the Princess came to her father to give him a kiss and immediately . . . she too changed into gold.

"Oh! what a dreadful thing!" he cried.

The King went back to the magician and asked him, "Please rid me of my magic touch! My darling daughter has turned into a golden statue, and I have not eaten for three days. Please turn my daughter back into flesh and blood, she is worth more to me than all my treasure!"

The magician waved his magic wand and turned everything back to its original state.

And King Midas understood that gold does not bring happiness. So he distributed his treasures amongst the poor and that was when he came to know true happiness.

THE UGLY DUCKLING

There was once a farm where some little ducklings were hatched in the corner of the barn.

They came out of their shells which they broke with their little beaks. But there was one . . .

. . . who when he presented himself to his Mummy Duck gave her such a shock that she cried, "What an ugly little duckling you are!"

All his little brothers laughed at him and teased him because he was so ugly.

He was so different from the others that they would not even let him have anything to eat. When he came near they cried, "Be off with you! You are too ugly to stay with us!"

Nobody loved him.

"I really am very ugly!" said the duckling, looking at himself in the waters of the lake. And he wept bitterly.

Poor little ugly duckling! How sad and unhappy he felt!

"Everybody hates me and avoids my company!"

As nobody understood him, he decided to leave home.

He went through the wood in search of a solitary spot where no one would laugh at him.

In the wood, he came to an empty house, where he spent the whole winter.

"Although I shall be all alone, nobody will laugh at me here," said the duckling to himself.

When spring came he went out for a walk.

He came to a lake and there he saw a majestically beautiful duckling and fell in love with her at first sight.

But when he jumped into the water to follow her he saw his own reflection there. What a marvellous surprise!

He was not an ugly duckling any longer. He was a handsome swan! Now he understood why he was so different from the little ducks he believed to be his brothers.

They got married and had some lovely little cygnets, who never felt miserable among their own kind.

The little tailor in our story was very happy in his work, but the flies buzzing all around him would not leave him in peace.

"One day I shall get so cross that these nasty little insects will get what's coming to them," said the little tailor.

That day came.

He got so cross that he seized a fly-swat and went for the flies, hitting six of them.

"I have killed six with a single blow!" cried he loudly.

At that precise moment there were two old ladies talking outside the tailor's window about the wicked giant who was terrorizing everyone and eating up all their crops.

The old ladies thought the tailor meant he had killed six giants.

The rumour quickly spread and reached the ears of the King, who sent for him and ordered him to kill the wicked giant.

No one took any notice of the little tailor's explanations, for they all believed he was a giant killer.

But when he arrived at the giant's castle and peeped in at the window, he received an impression of tremendous size.

"What an enormous man he is! No wonder he has been eating everything up. How on earth can I overcome him?"

He thought and thought, and then our friend came to the conclusion that the best way of overcoming him would be to sew up his mouth. That would prevent him from eating and he would lose his strength.

When the giant was asleep after an enormous meal, he put his plan into practice.

The next morning, when the giant came down to breakfast, he could not open his mouth.

The tailor was hiding to see what would happen.

"Oh dear! What has happened to me?" wondered the giant.

The giant, although he was very big, was also very slow-witted, and could not undo his mouth by himself.

Then the little tailor came out of his hiding place and told him that if he did not publicly beg the forgiveness of the King, his mouth would stay sewn up and he would starve to death.

The giant did just that and promised never to eat anything that did not belong to him again.

THE THREE LITTLE PIGS

Once upon a time there were three little pigs. Two of them were very idle and built their houses of twigs and straw so that they could get the job done quickly and sing all day long.

While the other little pig worked, how he worked!

One day, when they were completely absorbed in their singing, who should appear, but the wolf!

"We must run home!" cried the two terrified little pigs.

The little pigs ran away to hide somewhere safe from the big bad wolf.

"How plump and tender they will be!" said the wolf licking his lips in anticipation.

When they arrived at their little house, the pigs closed the door and thinking they were safe, leaned out of the window.

"Who's afraid of the big bad wolf, the big bad wolf!" they sang confidently.

At first the wolf was disconcerted, then he noticed how fragile and badly made their house was, and he huffed and he puffed and he blew their house down.

The two little pigs, on finding themselves with no shelter, fled in terror to the house of their brother.

"Quick brother! Open the door, the wolf is after us!" they cried.

Their brother barely had time to open the door to let them in and close it behind them.

No sooner had the little pigs entered when he shut the door right on the nose of the wolf. As soon as he had recovered from the blow, the wolf stood in front of the little house and said to them, "You can get ready to run. I am going to blow your house down like I did last time!"

So he huffed and he puffed, and he puffed and he huffed, but to no avail, and he fell down exhausted on the ground. He could not blow down the little house made of bricks and mortar that the hard-working little pig had built so well.

From that time onwards, the two lazy little pigs understood that work should come before fun and games.

LITTLE PIGTAILS

Once upon a time there was a pretty little Indian girl who liked to get up early and go into the wood to play with her friends, the animals.

One day, she was sailing her canoe on the river.

"Hello there!" said the friendly fishes.

Little Pigtails, for that was her name, was very happy and contented to have so many tiny friends.

They loved her very much and always gave her presents of wild flowers.

"Oh what a pretty daisy!" cried Little Pigtails.

Little Pigtails always went home with her arms full of bunches of flowers. It was the only way the animals had of thanking her for taking care of them and curing their ailments with her magic medicines and ointments.

"Is your little tummy better?" she asked the baby hare.

119

One day, when she was helping a little snail who had twisted his horn, a rabbit came up to her and she said to him, "What is the matter Loppy! Why are you so frightened?"

"Please help us!" he asked.

The rabbit explained to Little Pigtails that he was afraid because he had seen a hunter with a big gun who was going to shoot everything in sight.

Little Pigtails cried when she saw the dreadful things that the hunter was doing.

When she saw him wound the foot of a little bird, she could not contain herself and said to him, "What do you think you're doing? Don't you feel sorry for these poor defenceless little animals?"

And the hunter hung his head in shame, for he knew the little Indian girl was right.

"I'll never do it again," replied the hunter who was truly sorry.

"Oh no!" said the little girl doubtfully. "And the gun. What do you need that for?"

"Take it!" cried the hunter. "Go and throw it in the river. Then you will believe me!"

The hunter, who had been so wicked, understood that it was not right to kill defenceless little animals.

From that day forward, not only did he never do anybody any harm, but he became Little Pigtails's friend and helped her to look after any animals who had suffered mishaps and . . . I nearly forgot! They cured the wounded foot of the little bird and he flew away.

THE ELVES AND THE SHOEMAKER

Once upon a time there was a shoemaker who was so very poor that he could not afford a single piece of leather to make shoes with.

He was so miserable, for he had hardly had anything to eat, that he went to sleep hoping that his luck would change the next day.

When he woke up the next morning, what a surprise! There on the floor was a lovely pair of shoes.

"I wonder who put them there?" said the shoemaker to himself.

When the first customer arrived and saw that lovely pair of shoes, he paid the shoemaker handsomely.

"Congratulations, my good man! These are the best and most beautiful shoes I have ever seen!" said the customer. My daughter will be so pleased when I give them to her for her birthday."

The next day, the shoemaker found another pair of shoes.

"How extraordinary! I shall never be poor again! But who could have put them there?" he wondered.

That night, the shoemaker hid in his workshop to see what would happen.

When he was dropping off to sleep, he saw some little elves energetically making more shoes.

"They must have been helping me! Poor little things, how cold they must be without any clothes in this weather!"

And to show his gratitude for the good
deeds they had done, the shoemaker went
to town and bought plenty of clothes to give
to the little elves.

That night, when the little elves arrived at the shoemaker's workshop, they were so pleased to see the lovely presents and to know that the shoemaker no longer needed them.

So off they went to find other shoemakers who were in need of their assistance.

From then on, the shoemaker and cobbler never lacked money to buy leather and so he was able to go on making lovely shoes.

THE HARE AND THE TORTOISE

One day, a hare who was very proud of his agility, made a suggestion to the slow tortoise, "Hello pal! How would you like to run against me in the forthcoming Olympic race?"

The tortoise thought the race was already lost, but she agreed to compete.

"One, Two, Three!"

They both set off at the same time, but the hare went like an arrow and the tortoise at her usual ambling pace.

The hare was so far in front of the tortoise that he thought it would be a good idea to have a rest and eat some nice fresh carrots he could see.

"Yum, yum! These are juicy!" said the hare, devouring one carrot after another.

Then, for dessert, he ate a few wild flowers and after his meal he had a little nap

"My poor friend the tortoise still has a long way to go before she catches up with me. I have plenty of time to win the race," said the hare to himself.

The tortoise was ambling slowly on, but very purposefully and without stopping for an instant.

She was making such a tremendous effort that large drops of perspiration were trickling down her face.

The hare, after his long nap, was smugly making for the finishing line.

He felt sure he would win the race . . . but he soon discovered his mistake.

The tortoise had slowly but surely succeeded in coming first.

This convinced the conceited hare that perseverance is, without doubt, a great virtue.

Little Red Riding Hood was a very pretty girl who wore a red hood that her grandmother had given her.

Grandmother lived by herself in her house in the wood. One day Little Red Riding Hood's mother said to her, "Take this basket to your grandmother, as she is ill. But take care not to talk to any strangers on the way."

At a bend in the path she was waylaid by the wolf who asked her, ''Where are you going to Little Red Riding Hood?''

''I am taking this basket to my grandmother who is ill.''

The wolf suggested they play a game and said to her, ''Let's see who gets there first. You can take the short cut and I'll stay on the path.''

Little Red Riding Hood agreed, and the wolf, whose intentions were of the worst, had sent the little girl by the longest route, so that he would get there first and surprise her.

When the wolf arrived at grandmother's house, he knocked at the door.

"Who is it?" asked the old lady.

"It is little Red Riding Hood."

"Come in, dear, come in, the door is open."

The wolf locked up Grandma in a cupboard, put on her clothes, and got into her bed.

A moment later Little Red Riding Hood arrived.

"Oh Grandma! What big eyes you have!"

"All the better to see you with my dear."

"What big hands you have."

"All the better to hug you with."

"What big teeth you have Grandma!"

"All the better to eat you with! Grr . . ."

145

And with that, the wolf pounced on the poor little girl and was about to eat her up.

Little Red Riding Hood screamed and screamed.

"Help! Help!"

And when they heard her cries, all the little rabbits in the wood came running.

The rabbits, because there were so many of them, and they were very brave, succeeded in overcoming the wolf and releasing poor Little Red Riding Hood from his clutches.

And that is how the wolf completely lost his appetite for little girls.

Her Grandma was released safe and sound, and Little Red Riding Hood learned to do as her mother told her, because if she had done that in the first place, she never would have found herself in the clutches of the bad wolf.

HANSEL AND GRETEL

There was once a very, very poor woodcutter, who lived in a forest with his wife and his two children Hansel and Gretel. One day their stepmother, for she was not their real mother, told her husband that they ought to abandon them in the forest, for that way the small amount of food they had left would all be for them.

Their father was persuaded and they abandoned the children in the forest. But Hansel, who was very bright, was dropping crumbs of bread along the path, so that they would be able to find their way home.

That night they slept and at dawn they looked for the crumbs of bread, but they did not find any, for the birds had eaten them up.

They walked and walked, lost in the immense forest, and in the very deepest part of it, they came upon a pretty little house.

"Look Gretel! A little house! Perhaps they will give us something to eat and let us rest."

When they came near to the little house, they realized that it was made of candy, cakes and chocolate.

They were so hungry that they started to eat the bricks made of chocolate and candy, stuffing them in greedily.

"Isn't this nice?"

But, suddenly, out of the house came a witch.

"What's going on here? Who is eating my house?"

She was a wicked witch who had built the house with sweetmeats to attract the children so that she could eat them up.

That was how Hansel and Gretel fell into the trap laid by the wicked witch, who shut Hansel up in a cage and gave him lots of cakes to eat to fatten him up for the pot. She set Gretel to work helping her in the kitchen, but she was intending to eat her up too.

Days went by and when the witch saw that Hansel was not getting any fatter, she decided to cook him and eat him. The little girl was very frightened when she saw the fate that awaited her little brother. But she was a brave little girl, and when the witch was not looking, she gave her such a mighty push that she landed in the pot.

That is how Hansel and Gretel escaped from the witch. Then the two children ran away and found the path that led back to their house.

Their father was very happy to see them, for it was their stepmother who had abandoned them, and the three of them lived happily ever after.

In a little town called Hamelin, there had come to live all the rats that ever were and ever will be. They had taken over and made themselves masters of all the food in the town.

The Queen of that town was very mean and did not want to spend any money to get rid of the plague of rats. All she did was wail and moan in alarm, "How terrible! They are even taking my food!"

Finally, one day, the Queen sent for a man who was famous for making rats disappear with his magic pipe and said to him, "I, Queen of Hamelin, promise you a purseful of gold if you can rid me of these rats!"

The man agreed to the Queen's request and played his pipe.

The rats, bewitched by that magic sound, followed him to the river where they all drowned.

When there was not a single rat left in the town, the piper went to the Queen to collect his reward. But then, the Queen, who really was a miser, did not wish to keep her promise.

"Be off, I shall give you nothing!" said she in haughty tones.

"I shall avenge myself for this injustice," replied the man, very angry indeed.

And with that, he played his magic pipe and, at that sound all the children came running out of the town. Without ceasing his piping, he led them to the mountain, where he imprisoned them in a very deep cave, the existence of which was known only to him.

And that was his revenge on that miserly Queen.

Time went by and Hamelin became a sad and lifeless town. Even the flowers looked shrivelled and faded. An awful silence invaded the streets and schools and gardens. They were missing the happy laughter of the children!

The parents of the children went to see the Queen and asked her to pay her debt to the piper. For they could not do without their beloved children.

The Queen had no alternative but to keep her promise, and the piper released the children from their prison, bringing back smiles and happiness to the town of Hamelin.

From that day forward the miserly Queen always paid her debts.

SNOW WHITE AND ROSE RED

In a little house, there lived two sisters who were orphans. The elder was called Snow White and the younger was called Rose Red.

One night when it was very cold, there came a knock at the door of their little house. It was a great big bear, who was shivering with cold and asked if he could come in and warm himself a little by the fire.

The little girls were very frightened to see him, but they felt sorry for him and let him in.

Time went by and the bear made
friends with the little girls. Every day
he visited them to see if they needed
any help.

One day, Snow White was walking in the wood when she came upon a dwarf whose beard was caught in the mouth of a fish.

She felt sorry for him and wished to help him escape, so she snipped off the end of his beard with a pair of scissors.

Instead of thanking her the dwarf was angry.

Another day, it was Rose Red who met the same dwarf, and on this occasion he had got his beard entangled in the trunk of a tree.

Without a moment's thought, she ran to his aid and cut the tangled beard, but the dwarf, instead of being pleased, flew into a rage.

Time went by and one day, when the two little sisters were walking in the wood, they came upon the dwarf, who was concealing a hoard of treasure.

On finding himself discovered, the dwarf chased the two little girls with a club and told them he would give them a thrashing if they tried to rob him of his treasure.

But the friendly bear, who had seen and heard everything that took place, ran to their aid and gave the dwarf such a beating that he went down on his knees and begged pardon of the two little girls, asking them to forgive him for his bad temper.

Suddenly, the skin of the bear fell to the ground and there appeared a handsome prince, who had been enchanted by the dwarf and could only escape if the dwarf begged forgiveness.

To show his gratitude, the prince invited the two sisters to come and live with his parents, the King and Queen in their sumptuous palace. They all lived very happily together.

FEARLESS JOHN

Once upon a time there was a very strong and robust boy who claimed he knew no fear. That is why they called him Fearless John.

One night, to test his valour, John went to the haunted wood and decided to sleep there. He was not afraid of the silence and solitude of that place.

The next day, he went to the Castle of Terror, with the intention of spending three nights in it, for whoever did that would marry the King's daughter.

On the first night, out came a family of
phantoms, but Fearless John went for them
with a club and sent them fleeing in terror.

The next night there appeared an enormous bear, who tried to catch Fearless John in his jaws, but our hero defended himself, leaving the animal vanquished and fettered within seconds.

On the third night, he found himself face to face with a furious dragon, but Fearless John, using his brain and his powerful fists, made the hideous monster run up and down and back and forth.

He made it spin round and run about that immense castle so many times that at last the dragon felt so dizzy that it fell senseless on the ground.

The King heard about the valour of this young man they called Fearless John, and knowing that he had come through all the trials that beset him in the Castle of Terror, he rewarded him by granting him the hand of his daughter, the beautiful Princess Lily of the Valley.

THE FROG PRINCE

Once upon a time, there was a King who had a beautiful daughter, who spent hours playing with a golden ball in the garden of the Palace. But one day, the golden ball finished up at the bottom of the lake and the little Princess was most displeased.

"What is the matter little Princess, why are you crying so?" asked a frog, sticking his ugly head through the plants growing out of the water.

"My favourite ball has dropped to the bottom of this lake," she replied.

"Don't cry any more, I will help you. But what will you give me if I fetch your golden ball from the bottom?"

"I will give you anything you ask," she replied at once.

The frog dived down and emerged with the ball between his hands.

"Take it," he said. "But remember your promise. I wish to be your friend, to eat from your plate and sleep in your house."

"Yes, yes!" cried the Princess as she went away.

The truth was that the little Princess was only thinking of getting back her ball and had no intention of doing as the frog asked. She thought he was an ugly frog in his loathsome dwelling in that pond and could not follow her to her beautiful Palace. But . . .

The next day, when she got up, the first thing the Princess saw was the frog, who was waiting for her.

"Be off, ugly frog. I don't want to see you," said she.

"I have come," said the frog, "so that you can keep your promise and that is why I am going to stay with you."

The King, who had heard all, said to his daughter that promises were made to be kept, and thus the frog stayed in the Palace.

He sat at the table next to the little Princess and ate from the same plate. The Princess could not swallow a morsel, and then the frog said to her, "I have had enough now, take me to your room to sleep, I am so tired."

The little girl was furious with the frog and picked him up as high as she could and dashed him violently to the ground. When the frog crashed to the floor he turned into a handsome young man.

The surprised Princess asked him who he was and he told her that he was a King of a distant country upon whom a wicked witch had laid a spell and until then he had been obliged to live as a frog in the pool, waiting for the spell to be removed.

The two young people married and reigned happily together for many years.

THE WIZARD OF OZ

One day Mary and her dog went to play in a wood. How happy they were running about, when a great storm arose and a strong gust of wind lifted them up and carried them through the air to a beautiful foreign land.

One of the extraordinary things they came upon was a tearful scarecrow who was crying because he could not hear his heart beating like all the children.

The scarecrow asked the little girl to take him to see the
mighty Wizard of Oz who could make his heart beat by
magic. Mary felt sorry for him and offered to take him there.
Soon after, they met a lion who was crying because he was
tame and everyone laughed at him.

The lion also wished to see the mighty Wizard of Oz. So they set off together, and soon came upon a rattlesnake who was sad because she could not rattle.

Mary invited her to go with them and told them they were going in search of the Wizard of Oz.

They went on for a long time, until night fell.

At last they arrived at the castle of the Wizard of Oz hoping that he would solve all their problems.

As soon as they arrived before the great wizard, they asked him to make their wishes come true. He took pity on them when he heard of their afflictions and uncorked a bottle from which came a cloud of magic vapour.

When this wonderful blue cloud touched them, all their wishes came true and they happily left the castle of the Wizard of Oz.

Mary and her dog were so tired after they had been running about all day in the wood that they fell asleep on a rock and — they dreamed and dreamed — of the wonderful adventures we have just related.

THE END

Other titles in this series

COLLECTION ONE